OAKDALE

THEATER

A SHOWCASE FOR LEGENDS

By

FRANCIS NICHOLAS DRISCOLL

ISBN (E-Book): 978-1-966167-12-9

ISBN (Paperback): 978-1-966167-13-6

i

FRANCIS NICHOLAS DRISCOLL

CONTENTS

PROLOGUE

I first discovered the Oakdale Theater in 1997.

I heard about them from buying tickets for The Meadows in Hartford, where I first saw The Who.

It's a theater which had just recently been upgraded at the time, so needless to say I was ecstatic to see another one of my favorite bands there, Jethro Tull!

The theater was formerly in the round, the stage, but there was a 4000 seat addition built onto it, making it spectacular.

Over the years I went to see a whole bunch of my favorite Artists there, making it very special to me, and in a wicked turn of events, I now live in a place where I can see the Oakdale from my front porch!

So it's a constant reminder of all the great times I

had there, and got me to thinking I should write this Book!

Please enjoy if you will, my experiences at

The Oakdale Theater!

I certainly did.

OAKDALE THEATER: A SHOWCASE FOR LEGENDS

FRANCIS NICHOLAS DRISCOLL

CHAPTER 1: JETHRO TULL

My first Band I saw at the Oakdale, was none other than the Legendary Jethro Tull!

I was very excited because my parents played their music a lot throughout my youth, but unfortunately I was only 27 years old at the time, I was with a guy named Jon for this show, he was one of the local Musicians I met in Onionville, where I was living at the time.

Our speculation of their being an Opening Act was wrong, so hanging out in the parking lot partying turned out to be a big mistake, due to I missed the first song which was Aqualung, then I missed the whole first set due to Jon had my ticket and went to the bathroom with it, and I got stuck in the Lobby!

FRANCIS NICHOLAS DRISCOLL

When I finally got down to the Orchestra where my seats were, I couldn't believe how beautiful the place was, I heard stories about Oakdale, but nothing prepared me for this, the acoustics were magnificent! Anyway, they started the Second Set with Bungle in the Jungle and a full Thick as a Brick, then a bunch of well-known tracks and Locomotive Breath as their conclusion.

I saw them again the very next year with my ex-wife Jan but if you choose to save money on tickets, you can get stuck behind a partition in the rear orchestra like we did, but I got to see him do Aqualung and a bunch of new material from the newly released J-Tull dot com Album, which was doing well because of the advent of the internet.

These were Concerts I wish I would have written the Set List to, I can't really remember all that was played from it being over 25 years ago, and I went to see Tull 8 times over the years, once in Jones Beach we had front row, in the rain! Seeing Tull at Oakdale will always be a special memory, the second time as well and they love playing Connecticut, I even saw their show at Mohegan Sun Arena when I got back here on what may have been their final Tour! So many great flute solos, cheers Tull.

This was not the whirling dervish Ian Anderson of Jethro Tull's past, as he had recently broken his leg before showtime. However, he played the show from a couch they had brought out on stage, depicting what a real Musician would do instead of cancelling the concert.

FRANCIS NICHOLAS DRISCOLL

CHAPTER 2: THE ARTIST

FORMERLY KNOWN AS PRINCE

Right after Tull happened, almost immediately,

Prince signed to play 2 shows in a row, the first on my

Birthday!

Back then, my Birthday still meant something to

me, as nowadays it really doesn't, so I took a trip down to

Wallingford to buy the tickets, the experience was a hassle,

there was a long line that stretched out into the front area

which is now known as the Dome, it was the original area

where the Concerts were performed, prior to the 4000 Seat

Addition that was constructed.

People were fighting for spots in line to get tickets,

it was ridiculous but worth the wait, as I finally got my 2

FRANCIS NICHOLAS DRISCOLL

tickets for me and Jan, and they had Prince's unpronounceable symbol printed on the face of the tickets!

Then, as the Concert grew closer, Prince himself postponed the 2 shows and basically merged them both into 1 Concert, on Sept. 14th, largely due to the fact that neither of the Concerts Sold Out, even though it was the Jam of the Year Tour in support of his new Triple Album Emancipation!

It started out as a big mess, people had tickets for the same seats and were told to just take whatever seat you can find, and somehow it settled down after the show started. Larry Graham opened it and was great, playing Sly Stone Classics and his big hit One In a Million You, then Prince took the Stage!

SETLIST

OAKDALE THEATER: A SHOWCASE FOR LEGENDS

Jam of the Year

Talkin' Loud and Sayin' Nothing

(James Brown cover)

Purple Rain

Little Red Corvette

Get Yo Groove On

Six

(Madhouse song)

The Most Beautiful Girl in the World

Face Down

When You Were Mine

The Cross

One of Us

(Eric Bazilian cover)

FRANCIS NICHOLAS DRISCOLL

Do Me, Baby

Adore

Insatiable

Scandalous

Sexy M.F.

If I Was Your Girlfriend

Piano set

Diamonds and Pearls

The Beautiful Ones

Girls & Boys

How Come U Don't Call Me Anymore

Take Me With U

Raspberry Beret

Encore:

Kiss

Gett Off

Flash Light

(Parliament cover)

Stomp

(God's Property cover)

When Doves Cry

I just did a Google Search and found the Set List!

One of the reasons this Concert was very special was due to the fact that Prince found Religion after this show, so it was the last time things like Sexy MF and Face Down were ever played again! And Purple Rain being so high up in the Set list, I remember being astonished that he only sang the first verse and went right into the Guitar Solo,

and it was also the first time I saw Prince after my accident,

in a wheelchair, my seats were next to the Sound Board,

which I didn't know what that was at the time, and it blows

my mind that over the years, it was because of Prince's

influence over me that I became a Musician myself and

built a Recording Studio like he did, AND I became an

Audio Technology Major in College and eventually started

working on Solid State Logic Mixing Boards like the

Sound Board I was next to at the Oakdale that night, it was

also one of the last nights I saw him do the splits in honor

of James Brown!

I still have the shirt I bought that night.

Rest Easy Prince.

Thanks 4 The Years.

OAKDALE THEATER: A SHOWCASE FOR LEGENDS

FRANCIS NICHOLAS DRISCOLL

OAKDALE THEATER: A SHOWCASE FOR LEGENDS

CHAPTER 3: THE MOODY

BLUES

So, onward and upward, the next 2 Oakdale

Concerts we went to, in 1999 and 2000, were the fabulous

Moody Blues!

Seeing them for the first time after hearing them my

whole life was quite a thrill, flute player Ray Thomas was

still alive and in the band at the time, and performed

Timothy Leary's Dead, one of the shows highlights along

with Knights In White Satin and obvious classics like

Tuesday Afternoon....

I did see them one other time in Las Vegas at the

Hard Rock, it was a different Concert with the Days of

Future Passed Album performed in its entirety! Their music

OAKDALE THEATER: A SHOWCASE FOR LEGENDS

was quite transcendental, I was honored to have

experienced them and Oakdale was the perfect venue.

The Voice

Tuesday Afternoon

For My Lady

English Sunset

Words You Say

Strange Times

Steppin' in a Slide Zone

Haunted

The Story in Your Eyes

Second Set

Your Wildest Dreams

FRANCIS NICHOLAS DRISCOLL

Isn't Life Strange

The Other Side of Life

Nothing Changes

I'm Just a Singer (In a Rock and Roll Band)

Nights in White Satin

Legend of a Mind

Question

Encore:

Ride My See-Saw

OAKDALE THEATER: A SHOWCASE FOR LEGENDS

FRANCIS NICHOLAS DRISCOLL

CHAPTER 4: SANTANA

Looking back, one of the most interesting shows I saw at Oakdale was Santana, as it was my first time seeing them, the Supernatural Tour.

Over the years, after that night, I ended up seeing Santana 9 times after that in Hartford and then Las Vegas! Met Carlos Santana himself at The Joint in the front row one night, then I met every other member of the Band at one show or another!

It got to the point that I would come home with an autographed souvenir every time I went to see them! I saw them at MGM Grand Garden Arena, The Joint a bunch of times, and House of Blues Las Vegas a bunch of times!

FRANCIS NICHOLAS DRISCOLL

Also, over all those years since I saw them at

Oakdale, I've heard them perform each and every one of

their Albums!

The fact that their still around and still my friends is

amazing.

Spiritual / (Da le) Yaleo / Hannibal

Europa (Earth's Cry, Heaven's Smile)

Right On / Get On

Day of Celebration

Victory Is Won

Put Your Lights On

Africa Bamba

Maria Maria

OAKDALE THEATER: A SHOWCASE FOR LEGENDS

Love of My Life

Smooth

Bacalao con pan

Make Somebody Happy / Get It in Your Soul

Black Magic Woman / Gypsy Queen

Oye cómo va

(Tito Puente cover)

Everybody's Everything

Migra

Jingo

Prior to moving back to Connecticut from Las Vegas, I had this incredible Santana Experience at the House of Blues where they bumped me up to the Foundation Room, which is the very Last Row, but not what you think:

FRANCIS NICHOLAS DRISCOLL

Not only is it the best seat in the house, but the ambiance and surroundings of The Foundation Room is nothing short of spectacular, and then to top it off, when I moved back to Connecticut after my Mom's passing years ago, I got to see Santana at the Meadows in Hartford only this time with The Doobie Brothers in a 4 Hour Spectacular in which both bands even played together! Making my Santana experiences unbelievable, throughout my Life: Love you guys!

FRANCIS NICHOLAS DRISCOLL

CHAPTER 5: STING

Right around 1999 was when I was seeing all these shows there.

Sting had a new Album out called Brand New Day that was fabulous, the tickets were expensive so I got 2 in the Rear Orchestra, big mistake.

We got stuck behind a partition again.

Well, it didn't matter, because Sting is one of those kind of Artists, that whether he's singing, playing bass, piano or guitar, it's always spectacular!

The Set List Demographic was key in this show.

The first Set was also his solo stuff, which is great, but when he did Every Little Thing She Does Is Magic, and others from his Police Catalog, was when the place really lit up!

I did see him after that with The Police though, at Rentschler Field! There was nothing that could match the magic of the original trio.

A Thousand Years

If You Love Somebody Set Them Free

After the Rain Has Fallen

Perfect Love... Gone Wrong

All This Time

Seven Days

Fill Her Up

Fields of Gold

Every Little Thing She Does Is Magic

OAKDALE THEATER: A SHOWCASE FOR LEGENDS

Moon Over Bourbon Street

Englishman in New York

Tomorrow We'll See

Brand New Day

Roxanne

Encore:

Desert Rose

When the World Is Running Down, You Make the Best of What's Still Around

Every Breath You Take

Encore 2:

Message in a Bottle

Fragile

FRANCIS NICHOLAS DRISCOLL

CHAPTER 6: BLUES TRAVELER

The one time we went to see a Band there that we weren't too familiar with, was Blues Traveler.

Of course, we knew the hit Run Around, but I didn't know any of their other stuff, I knew John Popper was an outstanding Singer and great Harmonica Player!

They did a Charlie Daniels Band Cover, The Devil Went Down To Georgia, they were outstanding but it was long ago, I don't remember much more other than they were excellent!

But Anyway

Optimistic Thought

Johnny B. Goode

FRANCIS NICHOLAS DRISCOLL

(Chuck Berry cover)

The Devil Went Down to Georgia

(The Charlie Daniels Band cover)

Whoops

Believe Me

Crash Burn

Regarding Steven

What's for Breakfast

Jabberwock

Brother John

Set 2

Alone

Hook

Sweet Talking Hippie

OAKDALE THEATER: A SHOWCASE FOR LEGENDS

The Light in Her Eyes

The Joker

(Steve Miller Band cover)

NY Prophesie

Manhattan Bridge

Run-Around

Fucked Run

The Mountains Win Again

Go Outside & Drive

Maybe I'm Wrong

Hook

(reprise)

Encore:

Imagine

FRANCIS NICHOLAS DRISCOLL

(John Lennon cover)

FRANCIS NICHOLAS DRISCOLL

CHAPTER 7: EARTH WIND AND FIRE AND CHAKA KHAN

Sept. 11, 2001 was a horrible day for me, like most of us, but I lost my Uncle Joey that day.

On top of that, I was supposed to be closing on my first House that day in Bloomfield, which almost didn't go down, but I got it done, furthermore, I had tickets to see Earth Wind and Fire plus Chaka Khan that night!

The Oakdale started calling us up that afternoon, to ask if we wanted our money back, or if we would like to wait for a possible rescheduled date for the Concert, I couldn't even think about it.

The Show happened a week later, and as great as EWF and Chaka were, I don't remember much about it and there isn't even a set list or anything posted online, it was

something we needed due to the recent events but I felt as

though the Band struggled to get through the songs, as did

I.

Not my best Concert memory.

OAKDALE THEATER: A SHOWCASE FOR LEGENDS

FRANCIS NICHOLAS DRISCOLL

CHAPTER 8: YES

Another one of my favorite Classic Rock Bands I saw at Oakdale for the first time was Yes!

Now, Yes is one of these incredible bands that, like Tull, some of their songs go on for 20 minutes! So seeing them for the first time in a small theater like that, I didn't know what to expect....

They did 15 songs that went on for about 3 Hours!

I got punched in the throat by a drunk girl, it was just a rowdy crowd.

When we went to see the group Yes there, my Mom Virginia who has since passed away was there with us, as was her boyfriend Tommy who I consider my Stepfather, having them there made it all the more special to me, a

great memory.

OAKDALE THEATER: A SHOWCASE FOR LEGENDS

FRANCIS NICHOLAS DRISCOLL

CHAPTER 9: CHICAGO

We went to see a Chicago Christmas Show there.

Christmas songs were mixed in with all of Chicago's Classics, which was great, but I myself could do without all the Holiday stuff.

They're a very big Band, and Oakdale's Stage fit them well. A couple of years earlier, I got to meet some of them backstage at Jones Beach when they played there with the Doobie Brothers!

They were in top form.

FRANCIS NICHOLAS DRISCOLL

OAKDALE THEATER: A SHOWCASE FOR LEGENDS

CHAPTER 10: THE DOORS – 21ST CENTURY

We saw a Tribute Band featuring Ray Manzarek and Robbie Krieger of the original Band there, called The Doors of the 21st Century!

Of course, it was not Jim Morrison, but a singer named Ian Astbury, formerly of The Cult. However, they were amazing, and people were talking about how great this Concert was.

Roadhouse Blues

Break On Through (to the Other Side)

When the Music's Over

OAKDALE THEATER: A SHOWCASE FOR LEGENDS

Love Me Two Times

Moonlight Drive / Louie Louie

Horse Latitudes

Wild Child

Alabama Song (Whisky Bar)

Back Door Man

Five to One

The Crystal Ship

People Are Strange

Spanish Caravan

Maggie M'Gill

L.A. Woman

Light My Fire

FRANCIS NICHOLAS DRISCOLL

Encore:

Riders on the Storm

Peace Frog

Encore 2:

Soul Kitchen

OAKDALE THEATER: A SHOWCASE FOR LEGENDS

FRANCIS NICHOLAS DRISCOLL

CHAPTER 11: BB KING BLUES FESTIVAL

Ok, so when we went to see BB King, he goes:

I'm old enough to play the guitar sitting down if I want to.

And that's exactly what he did!

I don't remember a lot about it other than it was spectacular, Buddy Guy played also, as did Kenny Wayne Shepard who we missed out on.

Not too long after, BB passed on, and I will always be grateful to have seen this Legend of an Artist.

FRANCIS NICHOLAS DRISCOLL

CHAPTER 12: TODD RUNDGREN, ANN WILSON AND JOHN ENTWISTLE: A WALK DOWN ABBEY ROAD

One time it was crazy.

Todd Rundgren, Ann Wilson and John Entwistle did a show there called A Walk Down Abbey Road!

The Main Thing about it was Beatles Tribute Tracks, Todd played Revolution and While My guitar Gently Weeps, but he also did his own material, Hello Its Me, Bang On The Drum All Day etc.

John Entwistle did My Wife and was outstanding, he died shortly thereafter, Ann did Crazy On You and

Barracuda, and the rest was mostly all Beatles tracks, I

wish I would have taken down a Set List because I can't

find one these days for this Show.

OAKDALE THEATER: A SHOWCASE FOR LEGENDS

FRANCIS NICHOLAS DRISCOLL

CHAPTER 13: ALLMAN BROTHERS BAND

One of my oldest, favorite Bands that I was lucky enough to see at Oakdale, in 2004, was The Allman Brothers Band!

Now, the Allman Brothers are a Band I listened to in different stages of my Life.

The first was my Birth and my Youth, ABB came out in '69 and I was born in '72, so growing up in NYC their music was everywhere! In the late '80s they broke up, but in the '90s they made a huge comeback, and when they did, one of their favorite places to play was the Meadows Music Theater in Hartford, so, needless to say I rediscovered my favorite Band!

I also started going to see them at The Beacon Theater on Broadway, and the shows they put on there were 3 Hour Spectaculars in big clouds of Medical Marijuana, and that became my venue of choice to see them at, until they kicked Dickey Betts out of the Band!

Even after that, Warren Haynes rejoined the Band, along with Butch Trucks' nephew Derek, and they kept on rocking! In '03 I think it was, they put out a great new Album called Hittin' The Note, and after seeing them at the Beacon again, we decided to check them out at Oakdale in '04, I remember it well because the tye dye I bought said ABB 2004 Campaign in red white and blue!

It was a rowdy, Sold Out crowd, but what a fantastic show, I saw them about 10 times total, and since they've disbanded, we lost Gregg Allman, Dickey Betts AND Butch Trucks, leaving Jaimoe as the sole founding member alive, they reunited once at

OAKDALE THEATER: A SHOWCASE FOR LEGENDS

Madison Square Garden for the Blu Ray DVD Recording entitled The Brothers, which leaves me with hope that we might see them once again, although I'll certainly never forget seeing them at Oakdale.

I will love you guys forever, your Midnight Rider

Frankie Driscoll.

You Don't Love Me

Statesboro Blues

Wasted Words

Who's Been Talkin'

Hot 'Lanta

Old Before My Time

No One to Run With

FRANCIS NICHOLAS DRISCOLL

Woman Across the River

Set II

Revival

Come and Go Blues

Desdemona

Good Morning, Little School Girl

The High Cost of Low Living

Hoochie Coochie Man

Dreams

Instrumental Illness

Encore:

Southbound

64

OAKDALE THEATER: A SHOWCASE FOR LEGENDS

The Allman Brothers Band are HUGE in Connecticut, Jaimoe lives here and they played concerts here all the time, therefore making the one they did at Oakdale very, very special to me

Cheers Brothers, Please Come Home.

If you change your mind.

Oakdale needs one more show.

FRANCIS NICHOLAS DRISCOLL

OAKDALE THEATER: A SHOWCASE FOR LEGENDS

CHAPTER 14: MARIAH CAREY

This next Chapter is dedicated to Steve Mazz, my Uncle who passed away recently, who went to the Mariah Concert at Oakdale with me.

Rest Easy Stevie.

Ok, it was the 2003 Charmbracelet Tour. This was not my first experience seeing Mariah though. Me, my Wife and both her kids went to see her at Madison Square Garden when Missy Elliot and Da Brat were her supporting acts, but she was by herself I think on this Tour Stop.

To me, Mariah Carey is worthy of the Rock and Roll Hall of Fame, no question about it.

However, I remember that she was great, and she did an eclectic mix of her hits and new songs, but I just can't remember any specifics about it due to not being able to find a Set List....

I will say this though, if I was ever able to produce an All Star Concert at the Oakdale I would without a doubt choose the great Mariah Carey as one of the Headlining Acts!

When I was growing up, my favorite singer was Minnie Riperton, because she hit all the high notes, not to mention she was discovered and produced by Stevie Wonder!

Then, sometime in the '80s I believe, she succumbed to cancer and passed away, heartbreakingly. I remember I was devastated.

Mariah was the only female artist since then, that can hit the high notes like Minnie did, and moreover she's cranked out album after album, what Minnie would have done if she lived, and Mariah by now has released at least

15 albums I think, I believe it's a travesty that she's not in the Rock and Roll Hall of Fame all these years, she belongs in there, and I just wish that she'd perform Minnie's songs, and I would wish to see her perform with all these Artists at the Oakdale in a Headlining Capacity!

Plus she's The Most Beautiful Girl in the World, I Love You Mariah Carey! <3

OAKDALE THEATER: A SHOWCASE FOR LEGENDS

FRANCIS NICHOLAS DRISCOLL

CHAPTER 15: BEACH BOYS AND

THE RASCALS

Some places have sentimental value to me and Oakdale is certainly no exception.

With that being said, my friend Jana and I managed to somehow score 2 tickets in the Front Row for The Beach Boys and The Rascals Concert there recently!

I have seen The Beach Boys before this, but never The Rascals and never from this kind of close up perspective. Felix and the Rascals were great, even though they didn't do How Can I Be Sure? Which is my favorite song of theirs, they ran through their Hits and set the Stage for The Beach Boys!

Now, the Beach Boys aren't my favorite Band out of everyone I've seen at Oakdale, but they were around in the days of the Beatles, Stones and the Who, also if there was to ever be a Concert with all the acts I've seen at the Oakdale, The Beach Boys may very well get the Headlining Spot due to their 30 Song Sets and having been around the longest!

I had the Set List but couldn't find it, I do remember Oh Darlin' which was my favorite, Wouldn't It Be Nice, Sloop John B, California Girls, Good Vibrations, Surfer Girl, Surfin' Safari, I Get Around, Kokomo, God Only Knows, Don't Worry Baby, a huge chunk of the Hits were played! Outstanding, and while my other Oakdale Concerts were decades ago, this was just last year!

OAKDALE THEATER: A SHOWCASE FOR LEGENDS

FRANCIS NICHOLAS DRISCOLL

CHAPTER 16: THE BACK COVER

The Cover Perspective Photo Shot to this Book is quite extraordinary due to its meaning, and also has a lot to do with why this Book was written!

I had a very rough year last year, I had to move to a new place of residence called Skyview and when they brought me in on the stretcher, because I had to leave my wheelchair in a parking lot in Wethersfield, when I was brought in I didn't see any of this place's grounds or surroundings.

So when I got my wheelchair back, I started working immediately on weightlifting and various other forms of physical therapies. One day I was out on the front porch, and I had the most incredible epiphany:

FRANCIS NICHOLAS DRISCOLL

The Oakdale Theater can be seen right from my porch, only 2 blocks away!

FRANCIS NICHOLAS DRISCOLL

CHAPTER 17: IN CLOSING –

DIVINE INSPIRATION

In the past 3 Months here at Rehab, I worked so hard that I gained 15 pounds of muscle!

I also came to the conclusion of what a piece of heaven Skyview really is, when one day, from the porch, I could see the sun rise in the east and set in the west during the course of the day, like the name, complete with the Oakdale Theater in the background, it's the most beautiful Skyview I've ever seen, and very inspirational.

FRANCIS NICHOLAS DRISCOLL

OAKDALE THEATER: A SHOWCASE FOR LEGENDS

CHAPTER 18: LINKS, CONTACT

INFO AND RESUME

Facebook.com/Francis.Driscoll.7

Insagram: @qazeoneaownsa

Twitter (X): @thefrancissound

Qazeoneaownsa@aol.com

702 374 5837

FRANCIS NICHOLAS DRISCOLL

Wallingford, CT

702-374-5837

QAZEONEAOWNSA@AOL.COM

OBJECTIVE

To apply for any and all work positions.

EDUCATION

The Art Institute of Las Vegas-Dean's Honor Roll Student

TECHNICAL SKILLS

Programs: General: Technical:

FRANCIS NICHOLAS DRISCOLL

Apple (Mac)	Word	Mixing
Pro Tools 10	Excel	Mastering
Logic Pro 9	Power Point	Recording

ACHIEVEMENTS

ADMINISTRATOR: Francis Studios, 15 Years, Full and Current Owner

VEGAS DAYZ: Completed my first full length Album on CD of Original Compositions, available on TIDAL, Spotify, YouTube etc.

THE FRANCIS SOUND: Composed, recorded and released a full DVD of Music Videos.

Designed specific floor plans and completed two brand new, fully handicapped accessible Luxury Homes.

OAKDALE THEATER: A SHOWCASE FOR LEGENDS

Completed 6 Books: Prince: The Concert Chronicles+, Wonderlove Experiences, 2Pac 4Evr, The Las Vegas Return Story. The Evolution of Purple Reign, and Oakdale Theatre! Available at Amazon.com and wherever Books are sold!

REFERENCES

Johnny Juice Rosado: Producer, Public Enemy, Layup Studios-(516) 410-2962

Thomas Bitetto: Mechanic, Business Associate-(718) 208-6269

FRANCIS NICHOLAS DRISCOLL

OAKDALE THEATER: A SHOWCASE FOR LEGENDS

CHAPTER 19: EPILOGUE

The Oakdale Theater is one of those inspirational, magical places I'll never forget, and my dream is to put a Concert together there with all these Artists, to be filmed there for a Movie!

AND the reason I saw all these great Artists is because of a Promoter named Jim Koplik, who I've never met, but I've seen him drive into the Meadows in his spectacular Jaguar, and he's without a doubt the best Rock Promoter in history, and it's my dream to work for him! And I'm just 2 blocks up the hill currently. Wow.

When I ended up in Skyview, I didn't know what to expect, but once I started working out therapeutically, and when I ever saw The Oakdale in the near distance from the front porch, the divine inspiration was overwhelming, and meeting new friends like Scott here, I have tears in my eyes, thank you for believing in me, you guys! When I get back to Las Vegas, or whatever path I choose to follow in Life, I promise I won't let you down! Love Francis.

AND if Jimmy Koplik ever reads this Book and/or any of my others, my dream is to perform these Books Live one day, so if you like what I did, omg I live 2 blocks up the hill from your Office at the Oakdale! Please hit me up if you think I got what it takes to perform on your Stage, because all the years of being with Prince, The Allman Brothers etc. I know I do! And if we can get all these artists together for a show, it would reach epic proportions on the level of Woodstock, and would make a Monster of a Blu Ray DVD!

Jim Koplik is by far the very best rock and roll promoter, and music overall, for that matter, and I'm honored that I got to see all these wonderful shows thanks to him. Thanks Jim!

FRANCIS NICHOLAS DRISCOLL

Francis

Skyview Rehab

Up the block!

702 374 5837

OAKDALE THEATER: A SHOWCASE FOR LEGENDS

FRANCIS NICHOLAS DRISCOLL

CHAPTER 20: SPECIAL THANKS

Jana

Octavia

Kadeem

Amethist

Cindy

Nancy

Deanna

Lee-anne

Trey

Chanel

Ali

Kelly

FRANCIS NICHOLAS DRISCOLL

Joe

Jess

And all the rest of the employees and residents at

Skyview Rehab!

OAKDALE THEATER: A SHOWCASE FOR LEGENDS

FRANCIS NICHOLAS DRISCOLL

DISCLAIMER

This Book is a work of Fiction.

Any similarities to actual people or occurrences contain therein are purely coincidental.

I made it all up from my spectacular, vivid imagination!

On God as my witness.

Amen.

THE END